Once upon a time, there was a boy named Lucas.

Lucas was a very curious little boy.

He loved to learn new things at school

and try new games and sports.

Unfortunately, he really didn't like

to try new foods at dinner time.

Especially not fruits and vegetables!

What Lucas loved was Meatballs.

He loved meatballs so much that

he would prefer to eat them on anything.

Every time his mom made a meal

for the family, she had to plan it

around Lucas's love for meatballs.

Meatballs with rice, meatball soup,

meatball sandwiches, meatball pancakes,

and even meatballs on cereal!

He didn't care how weird it sounded.

He just really loved meatballs!

All his friends called him

The Meatball Monster!

One day his mother went to the store

to buy some meatballs, but the store was all out.

"*You ran out?*" asked the mother.

"*Yes, but we will be getting a new*

shipment tomorrow afternoon.

" said the store clerk.

"*Oh no!*" said the mother.

"*What is my boy going to eat for dinner tonight?*"

The mother looked at the store clerk

with a scared look. She went home worried,

and then suddenly she had an idea.

She called all the neighbors,

and her friends family,

to find out if anyone had extra meatballs

that they could spare. Her neighbors all said

"*No, I'm all out.*".

Her friends said the same.

But her sister said she had a full bag left over

because her kids loved them too.

So Lucas's mother offered to pay for

the extra bag of meatballs and picked it up that day.

She was so lucky to find someone

who had meatballs for her son!

Meanwhile at the park Lucas played with friends

who were talking about other things they liked to eat.

Some loved hotdogs, and some loved corn on the cobb!

Some loved hamburgers, and some loved pasta!

They all talked about how they couldn't wait

to get home to eat whatever their mother was making.

They loved not knowing what their mother was cooking

so they could be surprised each evening.

That, of course, made dinner more exciting!

So curious Lucas thought that was

a great idea and that maybe he should

try something different also.

He went home and said *"Hey mom?"*

"Yes?" said the mother.

"I think it's ok if you don't make me meatballs

everyday. I want to be like my friends at the park.

They eat something different everyday

and they get excited to find out

what's for dinner. I want to feel that way too!"

"Really?" said the mother, *"I thought*

you would be upset if I made something different."

"*Well,*" Lucas said,

"*after talking to my friends at the park today,*

I think it's ok to try some other foods too.

It's just like learning, and I love to learn!

I bet that by tasting different foods,

I can learn to love even more foods!

I'm curious about how they taste,

and how healthy they are for me!"

"Very well." said the mother,

"From now on, I won't tell you

what I am making for dinner.

It will be a surprise! And while you eat,

I can tell you how healthy it is!"

"Yay!" Lucas exclaimed, "I can't wait

to tell my friends that I no longer eat just meatballs!"

Lucas thought about it for a moment and said

"You know what, mom?

I think I'm going to like trying new foods,

and I bet it will even make me smarter and healthier."

"*Absolutely!*" said the mother.

"*I'm so glad you changed your mind*

about eating just meatballs, because now

I can cook many other things too!"

said the mother.

So from then on, curious Lucas

was always excited to go home

and ask his mom "*What's for dinner!?*"

Lucas is a very smart and curious boy.

He loves exploring and learning new things all the time.

He has a passion for meatballs.

When he was still a baby his mother gave him some meatball sauce to taste.

Little did she knew that he would love meatballs too much!

As he grew older he would try a few different foods,

but his mom always had to include his favorite,

meatballs, in every single dish that she prepared for him.

One day, as he plays at the park with his friends,

Lucas overhears them talking about how much

they love going home and finding out what's for dinner each night.

They all share the excitement they feel as they wonder

what good foods they might get to taste that night at dinnertime.

The conversation, of course, makes Lucas curious.

He decides wanted to try it out and feel excited like his friends.

The curious boy learned that meatballs aren't the only good food around.

He learned that there are lots of other healthy and delicious choices to eat.

His mother was also relieved that he was finally more open to trying new foods!

Hi! My name is Memo and I am the dad of Peter. I was inspired to write this book by my son. Peter is now 7 years old and he loves bedtime stories. Ever since Peter was still a baby, my wife and I read to him before bed every night. As he began to grow he became more interested in bedtime stories. Every month we would buy new books to read to him, and family members would give him books for holidays and birthdays. Now, at 7 years old, he has a whole library of children's books. One night I was reading a bedtime story to Peter and he asked me "Hey daddy, why don't we create our own bedtime stories?" So I thought to myself, "Why not? It sounded like a great idea." The following day we sat in the living room, brainstorming our first little book together. We laughed at each other's ideas. Eventually, we came up with this story, about a curious boy named Lucas.

This book was written by my son and I at home, as we started to tell the story out loud as if someone was listening to us. I contacted my illustrator to ask if she could help our story come to life, and without any hesitation, she said "Yes!" My wife had no idea what my son and I were up to, so our book was a complete surprise to her! She loved our first draft though, and even came onboard at that point to help with some editing. This ended up being a really fun family project! So, here it is, the finished product...a story book that grew from a little idea! I hope you enjoyed this bedtime story as much as we have enjoyed writing it! We have a new book coming soon called

"I Wonder IF I Was a . . ."

Thank you for being supportive, and remember to _keep your imagination going_!

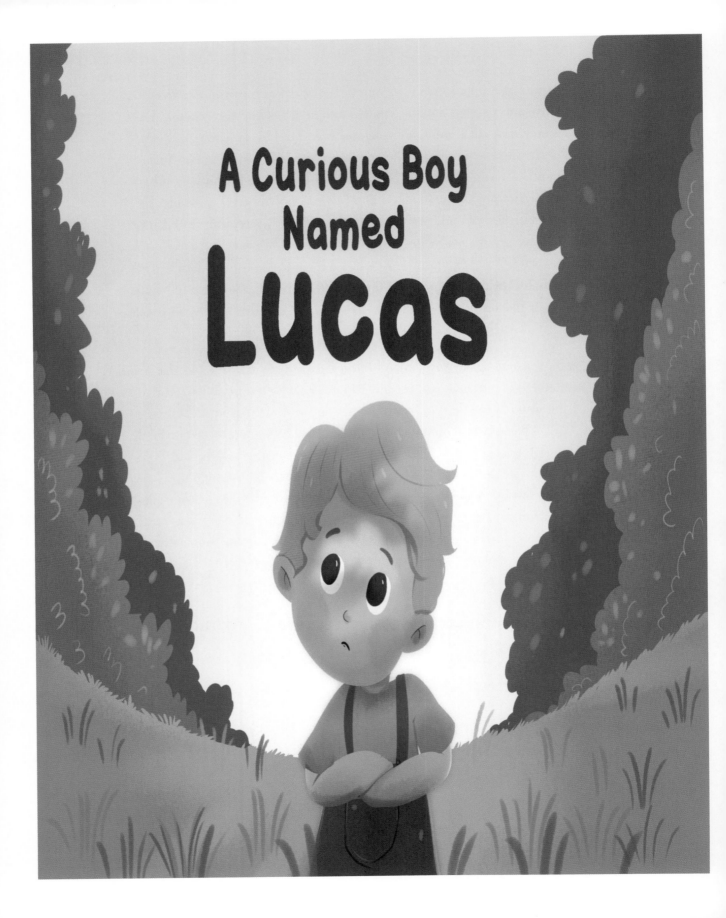

Printed in Great Britain
by Amazon

46987809R00016